Juliet's pun.

GEMMA ZA

JULIET'S PUNISHMENT

First edition. January 21, 2024.

Copyright © 2024 GEMMA ZAMORA.

ISBN: 979-8224676248

Written by GEMMA ZAMORA.

Table of Contents

Chapter 1
Preamble and presentations

BEFORE LAUNCHING INTO this story, I believe I must make a few introductions, and place the story in its context.

Juliet

I had the opportunity to present it at length, in the introduction to the story "48 Hours". I'm just going to repeat what I wrote about her as part of the challenge she gave me..

I had read, on a site exclusively publishing erotic stories, texts that she had written, under the pseudonym Pyjamanoir. She evoked, without taboos, a relationship of domination/ submission that she maintained with her companion, a certain...

Juliet.

At the time, even though I was a liberated woman who dared to put into practice some of her fantasies, I did not feel tempted by submission.

But Juliette's texts – well written – and perhaps the fact that one of the two protagonists has the same first name as me, aroused in me a little more than interest. A kind of excitement.

I felt the need to chat with the author, and I sent her a message, via the site in question, to tell her that I appreciated her stories and her style, and that the homonym with her heroine appealed to me. had troubled. There followed an exchange via the internet, which I will not recount here in detail.

Over the course of these emails, our conversations took an increasingly intimate turn. Especially since Juliette is bi, like me. We spoke very freely about our sex life and our fantasies, and she told me in detail about her relationship with Juliette – whom she called "her Juliette", to avoid confusion.

Strangely, I managed to identify with this other Juliette, when I read what Juliette wrote, and I felt a vague desire to know the pleasure that she obviously found in this relationship.

I opened up to Juliette, first in a roundabout way, then more and more frankly, until finally by him ask (I have shame When I'm there think again) if She would accept of initiate me "virtually" upon submission. An idea of a cerebral woman a little too focused on sex, no doubt... From that day on, Juliette began to give me orders, to impose a certain number of gestures on me And of attitudes. We were too much distant geographically to meet, but we engaged in hot chats on the net, to give more reality to this relationship, and "the other" Juliette sometimes participated in our games.

These games turned into challenges, pushing me to go further and further into submission, and Juliette often used and abused my exhibitionist inclination. We sometimes reversed roles, and I was Juliette's "mistress", but I admit that I was less talented than her.

Those who have read both versions of "48 Hours" (each of us having taken on the same challenge) know how far these games can take us...

Juliet

Juliette's companion. She is often the heroine of the many stories published here by her "Mistress".

"Juliet's Punishment" (which I advise you to read) is the starting point of this new text. I appear there, without Juliette having explicitly mentioned me. I wanted to give my version of this evening, which made me switch to hard SM.

Yvette

Neighbor and friend of Juliette. Juliette has been subjected – in turn, for several years – to her most extreme demands.

This woman's sexuality and her imagination know no limits, and she leads those who frequent her into the worst orgies.

Chapter 2

IT ALL STARTED WITH an email, which arrived in my voicemail, on a Monday. The sender – a certain Yvette – was unknown to me, and I hesitated to open it. Unless... What if it was Juliette's friend? In one click, I was fixed.

"Hello Juliette.

Juliette made me read the stories you publish on Sexecom, and the messages you exchange on the internet. I took the opportunity to note down your email address.

I have a proposition for you.

I know how much you love sex, and how Juliette knew how to lead you on the path of submission. You also have a penchant for SM, if I believe some of your stories. "A Hellish Night" is very revealing of what you accept or, if you have included some fantasies, of what you are ready to accept, more or less consciously.

If you will trust me, I will send you a telephone number, which you will call on my behalf.

You will then be invited to a party, which you will remember for a long time. And, to motivate you, a

No one you dream of meeting will attend.

I'm waiting for your answer. Yvette »

I remained doubtful for a long time. I knew Yvette's reputation, from what Juliette had told me about it. I had every reason to dread the evening she was offering me.

But my incorrigible curiosity tickled me dangerously...

And then there was that last, cryptic sentence. Who could the other participant – or participant – be at this evening? Juliet? It was unlikely, because she would probably have invited me herself...

For more than an hour, I thought and procrastinated. I was unable to concentrate on my work. My fears seemed more and more ridiculous. After all, I was an adult and, if I ever found myself in danger, I always knew how to get out of it.

Moreover, although I did not admit it to myself, the fact that the invitation came from this Yvette, of whom Juliette had painted a sulphurous picture for me, pushed me to accept, to be Juliette's equal.

So, I made up my mind, and I responded, tersely.
"Hello Yvette. I accept your proposal. Juliet »

A few minutes later, a new message from Yvette reached me, just as laconic. Just a first name, improbable – Laury – and a cell number, to call in the evening.

Chapter 3

THE DAY SEEMED LONG to me, and I kept thinking about this exchange of emails, which I reread several times. Who could this Laury be? What were his links with Juliette? And why had Yvette, whose reputation worried me, contacted me?

After my classes, I went home, and I moped around, fiddling with my smartphone. I was still hesitant. Then 7:00 p.m. appeared on the screen. It was now or never... I dialed Laury's number, who picked up on the third ring.

- Hello, Laury? Good evening. It's Juliette, I'm calling on behalf of Yvette.

- Good evening Juliette. I was waiting for your call.

The voice was hoarse, but not unpleasant, imbued with a certain sensuality. The tone was brief, authoritarian. I couldn't imagine the woman I was talking to.

- Yvette told me about an evening at your place, but she didn't tell me much more.

- I think she's told you enough for you to guess the nature of this evening. And Yvette told me a lot about you, especially about your sexuality and your taste for submission. She thought you would be a perfect guest at our next games, in which someone you know will be very... actively participating, and I trust her completely.

- Perhaps you can give me an idea of how it will unfold, I said in a voice so timid that it surprised even me.

- Apart from the fact that you will have an experience of submission and exhibition which will surpass anything you have known – and I know that you are not a novice – I will not tell you more. I won't teach you that uncertainty and surprise are part of these games.

- But... if what I have to endure is more than I can bear...

- We will agree on a word, which you will say in this case, to unambiguously ask us to stop. But know that, in this case, you will be immediately expelled from this evening, and you will incur the wrath of Yvette (probably also of Juliette). Is that clear, Juliette?

- Um... yes, Laury.

- GOOD. One last clarification: our evening takes place in a town on the tip of Brittany. You will have to make a long trip. Do you accept this invitation?

- Will you give me some time to think about it?
- No. You have to tell me yes or no. Right away.

I was panicked. No sound could come out of my tight throat. Never had I had the feeling of putting myself in danger with a simple yes. But I pulled myself together... There was this word, which would allow me to stop everything, if Laury and her friends crossed the line. So why not satisfy my curiosity, once again?

- It's yes, I replied after taking a long

inspiration.

- Perfect, said Laury, without showing any emotion. Our party will take place next Saturday, and you will have to arrive at our house at 11 p.m. sharp. I will send you by email our address and my instructions. Good evening Juliette.

- Good evening Laury...

I didn't have time to finish saying his name. She had already hung up.

I remained stunned. I had just realized that, throughout the conversation, I had addressed Laury, while she addressed me informally. This had never happened to me. I was already putting myself in a position of submission.

An hour later, an email arrived in my inbox.

The address I had to go to was almost a 4-hour drive from my house, and Laury advised me to get a room there.

The rest of the message was about my outfit. I will have to wear a short dress, buttoned in the front. I will leave the top buttons open, down to under my breasts, and the bottom ones down to my pussy. Underneath, I will be naked, with a blue Rosebud (how did she know I had one?) between my buttocks.

I will have to leave my room in this outfit... Finally, Laury asked me to

communicate the address of my room, as soon as I have remembered it.

Immediately, I started looking for a room or studio to rent, on Airbnb. I preferred this solution to a hotel room, out of discretion.

That same evening, I gave the address to Laury, who asked me to call him when I arrived to confirm my presence. Observe your talents as an organizer helped to reassure me.

Chapter 4

DURING THE WEEK THAT followed, I tried to contact Juliette by email, numerous times, to ask her if she could tell me something about that evening. At least reassure myself. But all my messages went unanswered.

The dreaded Saturday finally arrived, and I left for the tip of Brittany, taking in my car the dress and the anal jewel demanded by Laury. Apart from that, my luggage was light: a change of clothes, a toiletry bag...

Arriving at my destination late in the afternoon, I settled into my small studio, in which I ultimately only spent a few hours. As agreed, I called Laury.

- Good evening Laury. It's Juliette. I arrived safely at the apartment I rented.

- Perfect, you seem to be very obedient. A good point for you, Juliette. A taxi I know will pick you up at 10:30 p.m. Do you remember what outfit you should wear?

- Yes, Laury. A dress buttoned in the front, a piece of jewelry anal...

- Alright. Take advantage of the time you have left to have dinner and gain strength. You're going to need it!

As brief and authoritative as ever, Laury had already hung up, and I went out to look for a restaurant.

I found one, a few hundred meters away. The weather was nice, and the temperature was pleasant. I took the opportunity to eat on the terrace. A mixed salad, a dessert. I drank water, because I wanted to keep my mind clear, and I was afraid it would be a drunken evening.

I was back home before 9 p.m., I still had plenty of time to get ready.

I undressed in front of the large bathroom mirror and looked at my naked body, unable to help but fear what the guests at this party were going to do to it. I had spent holidays in the sun, and I had been able to get a full tan most of the time. Only the mark of a very small thong could be noticed by an attentive eye, and even then.

I took my shower, soaping myself for a long time with a scented gel. I combed my short hair into a messy style, to give myself a wilder look, and I put on makeup. A heavier makeup than usual. Especially my eyes and my mouth. A cream to soften the skin on my body a little more. And to finish, a heady and sensual fragrance.

I slid my fingers between my buttocks, after coating them with saliva. With the pad of my index finger, I gently massaged my little dark carnation until it relaxed. The tip of my finger forced my rosette, and slipped in, soon followed by my middle finger. I held back so as not to make myself cum, and I inserted my anal jewel into my little hole.

Then I put on my dress, in ecru linen, tight, in

scrupulously following Laury's instructions. The open buttons showed my free breasts, and my smooth pussy when I sat down. Fortunately I was not at the hotel: I imagined the effect produced by crossing the reception...

At exactly 10:30 p.m., my landing doorbell rang. I opened it, and found myself facing a tall, muscular black man with a shaved head. His broad shoulders held up his impeccable white shirt.

He paused briefly, examining me from head to toe, and I think I blushed, his gaze was so inquisitive. Then he said to me:

- Juliet? Good evening, it was Laury who asked me to come pick you up.

- Yes, it's me, good evening.
- Follow me.

He was hardly more talkative than the woman who had invited me, and the journey was made in silence. The car, a black Audi sedan, was comfortable, and we left the city, following a road that sometimes skirted the sea.

Then my taciturn driver parked in front of a large old bourgeois house, built on a hillock. He got out, opened my door, and watched me get out, without apparent reaction to my dress which was gaping over my breasts and my bare thighs.

I walked down a short driveway, which led me to an imposing wooden front door. I rang the bell, and a few seconds later, Laury greeted me.

She was a very beautiful woman, probably around fifty years old – I was expecting to find someone younger. Blonde, wearing a heavy bun that suggested long, thick hair, she seemed to be barely taller than

Me. Behind large glasses, his blue eyes sparkled with an expression passing without transition from the worst severity to the most exciting sensuality. Her makeup highlighted a luscious mouth.

She was dressed in a very tight burgundy suit, which hugged her full forms. She was very round, but she wore her curves well, and the jacket revealed the birth of an imposing chest. With her black stockings and her stiletto heels, she was the typical portrait of the dominant, upper-class woman.

- Good evening Juliette, she said. You are on time, dressed according to my instructions... Your docility will perhaps save you from some unnecessary suffering.

While speaking, Laury had uncovered my breasts, and rolled up my dress, to check that I was naked underneath, and that I was wearing my anal jewelry.

- Good evening Laury, I simply replied.

- I will take you to the large living room where our evening will take place, and introduce you to our other guests. Well, not everyone, because the person you know hasn't arrived yet. But already, I'm going to complete your outfit a little.

She took a red leather collar from a low piece of furniture, which she tied around my neck, and from which hung a short leash. I understood that I had just entered into my character as submissive and sexual object; shame and anguish returned to overwhelm me from that moment on.

Laury grabbed the leash, and pulled me to a double door, to access a huge room, with white walls and beams painted a light color. The room was so large that the chandeliers were insufficient to light it, and spotlights had been installed.

The furnishings were basic, but three large sofas and a huge wooden table sat on the middle of the room, and a giant screen occupied a section of the wall. But what I noticed right away was a large wooden Saint Andrew's cross, standing not far from the sofas.

- Let me introduce you to Maxime, my husband, said Laury in a ceremonious tone.

I was surprised by the appearance of the man, who seemed older than her. Around sixty. Thick gray hair, a white beard. He was dressed in a dark suit, and was milling around the giant screen, obviously trying to make a connection.

Three men, seated on the sofas, stared at me.

- Juliette, our little submissive slut for this evening, added Laury to introduce me to the trio. Yvette highly recommended her to me, and this girl spent almost four hours in the car to be dominated and fucked like a whore.

The three men were much younger. Probably in my thirties, like me. Perhaps less.

In the first, I recognized the driver who had brought me here. The second, blond, seemed less athletic than the black man – but that in no way predicted his sexual performance – and he too was wearing black pants and a white shirt. The last one had an impressive build and musculature, molded into a white polo shirt, and his long, black hair was pulled back.

I must admit that their virility did not leave me indifferent, and in any other context than this evening, I would not have refused their advances either.

- And now, Juliette, Laury continued, you are going to tell us the word you chose, to tell us that you ceases to be consenting, and that we must stop. I remind you that, in this case, you will be immediately expelled from this house, and banned from all our parties.

- *Panic*, I replied in a blank voice.

- Well, we'll remember that word, hoping we won't hear it. You still have to introduce yourself, let's say... physically. Take off your dress !

The tone was harsh, and I felt like I was a little girl again. A shame for a teacher! I began to slowly undo the few buttons that closed – although partially – my dress. All eyes were on me when my small breasts began to peek out in the halogen light.

I opened the sides of my dress wide, the fabric slowly slid down my arms and my body, and I found myself naked, perched on my heels. The comments began to flow, and I felt like a prisoner in a slave market, while Laury turned me around, to offer all the facets of my anatomy to lustful gazes.

- Very exciting, this petite girl, with her demure woman style, said one of the men. I can't wait to see her impaled on our cocks.

- Yes, adds Laury, you wouldn't say at first glance that she's a real slut, but they're the worst.

- I love her small breasts, with their sensitive tips, commented another man while kneading my chest. They are very firm, we want to torture them.

- And she's already wet, said Laury, pointing to her finger, glistening with wetness, which she had just passed between my thighs.

- This anal jewel is very pretty, said the one who had led me here. It will already be a little dilated on that side. Do you like being anal fucked, Juliette?

   - Answer it, Laury insisted.
   - Yes, I like it, I replied in a hushed voice.
   - Stronger ! Say you like being fucked!
   - Yes, I like being fucked.

My voice resounding in the huge room surprised even me. Just like the excitement that I felt coming over me, despite – or because of – the humiliation. Laury took my leash again, and led me to the cross of Saint Andrew.

She raised my arms, and tied them into the bracelets fixed on the upper branches. Then it was the turn of my ankles. I found myself torn apart, exhibited, delivered defenseless to the participants in this evening. And I had every reason to think that I was going to be their toy, their sex slave, for many hours.

Laury fetched a small precious wooden box from a piece of furniture, which she opened before my eyes. The content made me shudder...

She took the tip of one of my breasts between her fingers, pinched it, pulled it, until I winced in pain. Then she enclosed it in a stainless steel clamp, fitted with a screw, which allowed the pressure on my darting nipple to be adjusted. She squeezed, and very quickly, the pain reached the limits of bearable, but I felt a pleasure that I knew only too well.

A small smile of satisfaction lit up his face for the first time, and my second little tit suffered the same fate.

- I think you also love this kind of toy, she said to me, taking a vibrating egg out of the box. Isn't that right, Juliette?

   - Yes, Laury.
   - You see, I am well informed about your account.

She passed her hand between my thighs, opened my pussy with her fingertips, and presented the sex toy at the entrance to my slit. She slid it between my labia for a few moments, and when I let out a little moan, she pushed the egg suddenly, brutally, into my soaked cunt.

That's when the doorbell rang, and Laury left me and went back to the lobby.

Chapter 5

I REMAINED ALONE, TIED up, crucified, in front of the four men who never took their eyes off me.

I heard the heavy door of the house open, muffled voices, then the sound of approaching footsteps. Laury returned, accompanied by two other women with whom she was chatting, as if I did not exist.

The oldest was a redhead. She wore a white shirt, largely low-cut, over a green skirt. Despite her age, her body appeared to be that of a young girl, as far as I could tell.

She was holding another blindfolded girl by the arm. Definitely my age. Tall and muscular, very beautiful, with long brown hair. His outfit consisted of a long, open vest and large leather boots. Other than that, she was naked. A superb chest, long legs with sports thighs, a flat stomach... I had never met her, but her physique reminded me of someone.

    - Here it is finally, said Laury. Isn't she attached?
    - I didn't want to take that risk, replied the

redhead. There are people in town on Saturday evening. But I guess you have what you need, right?

- Obviously...

- Perfect ! Juliette is all yours! But be nice and wait until I get home. I don't want to miss any of the party.
- We will be patient, my dear Yvette, replied Laury's husband. We will wait to see you, comfortably seated next to Juliette.
In a flash, I understood everything. The redhead was Yvette, to whom I owed my presence here. And the young and pretty blindfolded brunette was none other than Juliette, my namesake, Juliette's companion. I had seen photos of her naked before, but her face was hidden in those photos. So she was the other guest that I knew!
- Speaking of which... Why didn't you give us your pretty Juliette, asked Maxime. Would you fall into selfishness?

- Where are you with the video, asked Yvette?

- Just start the connection. For what ? Yvette's arm circled Juliette's waist.

- I made sure Juliette didn't hear. It was she who asked me how to punish her dear Juliette, in an original way. When the connection is made, you can rinse your eye. I plan to make the most of Juliette. She is as obedient to me as Juliette is to her. And one day, I promise you, she will be here. Instead, this beautiful little slut Juliette.
- You spoil us, my darling, replied Laury with a little laugh. And this other "guest" that you sent us will undoubtedly also be a piece of royalty for this evening.

Yvette turned on her heel, went out, and Laury passed her

arm around Juliette's waist.

- My name is Laury... It's an old first name from Brittany. You like ?

- Yes... replied Juliette, and I discovered the sound of her voice, broken by anguish.

- It is charming Juliet. I like a lot. Do you havethirsty ? Water only, of course.

- Yes. Thanks Laury.

Juliette was blinded by the blindfold, and Laury placed a heavy glass of water in her hand.

- Drink everything, my dear! You'll need to hydrate, that's for sure. Don't hesitate to ask for a drink. This will be the only right that will be granted to you I believe... Ah! Are you afraid Juliette?

Juliette drank the glass of water in one gulp. Her breasts rose to the rhythm of her heavy breathing, and the spectacle of this humiliated girl, offered to strangers, began to excite me. I forgot that I had deliberately put myself in the same situation...

- Yes, replied Juliette.

- So stop with your unanswered yes...

- Yes I'm afraid...

Laury placed herself behind Juliette, and placed her hands on her shoulders, which she gently massaged through the wool.

- I will give you another choice. You choose to call me Laury, madame, or mistress... I'm listening to you Juliette.

- Laura.

- GOOD ! Don't forget to address me by calling me that. Or you will regret it. It's understood ?

- Yes.

- I'm not really convinced...
- Yes Laury. Pardon...
- I love that you ask for forgiveness, said Laury with

a small laugh, before continuing.

- I know you like to obey your wife. You see, I even know that you call Juliette "your wife." Do you think you'll like obeying me?

   - I don't know Laury...

Laury laughs again, caressing Juliette's cheek.

- I know it, my dear. And you'll tell me, you'll see... Another drink?

   - Yes, please Laury.

- You are adorable, said Laury, kissing Juliette on the cheek. I'll give you some explanations. You were good and you deserve me to be nice to you. Or maybe... Do you prefer not to know anything about what's going to happen to you?

   - I prefer to know... Laury.

Laury's hands slowly descended towards Juliette's chest. Then she insisted on her breasts, with her nails, before going up to her neck.

- Close your eyes, Laury whispered... Don't open them! Just long enough for me to put a proper mask on your face. Ready?

   — Yes... Laury.

She placed a thick leather mask on my namesake's face. He covered her eyes, and partly hid her cheeks. Then Laury spoke again.

- In front of you... A giant screen. What happens here will be broadcast on this screen. Your wife, Yvette, and other people, loving the joys of libertinage, will watch us. Seven couples in all. These people will see us taking care of you. Trustworthy friends of mine. You don't have to worry, they are very discreet. Discretion is essential in our environment. Like confidence. This is the first point. Questions ?

- No Laury.

- The installation is ready and I will notify you when we connect.

I understood better what Yvette and Laury had spoken about. Like the "other" Juliette, I was going to be exhibited, by video. I thought for a moment that I was going to realize one of my exhibitionist fantasies, which I refused to consider, out of caution: being filmed in an X-rated video...

While playing with Juliette's hair and stroking it, Laury continued her explanations, so that the pretty brunette could imagine what she could not see.

- We are in the large living room. It is a room of more than a hundred square meters. We wanted it that way. Upstairs is our house. We are not alone of course, you must have guessed. You heard Maxime talking with Yvette. It is my husband. Maxime and me, Simon, Vincent and Timothée. Three friends just as trustworthy as those behind our screen. Just as discreet and above all very... very helpful! Before Yvette and Juliette contacted us, we had planned a nice little evening. We didn't cancel it. So... We kept another little Juliette with us...

Laury guided Juliette across the room, and she made her approach me. She scratched her breasts, and pinched the nipples which stood up.

- It seems that Juliette is a name that suits little naughty girls. Our other guest has a name like you. It's your only resemblance or almost... Let's go see it! Well, it's just a way of speaking.

Chapter 6

LAURY'S NAILS PINCHED harder the nipples of poor Juliette, who held back a muffled complaint.

- Ah! Maxime signals to me that the connection is made... From now on, everything is published on our blog. I think you like being shown off, don't you?

   - It's the first time... Like this... Laury.

   - You're going to like being looked at, my dear. Trust me... What was I saying?

Juliette was now very close to me, and I couldn't help but admire her appearance. A real cannon! I found her even more beautiful than in her photos. Maxime untied one of my wrists, and Laury took my hand to place it in Juliette's.

Juliette's fear was palpable. Laury pulled her back, guiding her with her hands holding her axes tightly.

   - I said you only had your first name in

common, apart from a few small things. I speak for you Juliette...
Our little Juliette is not blindfolded and can see you. I'll explain to you
very quickly. You are both roughly the same age. You must be close to one
hundred and eighty centimeters and our little Juliette must barely exceed
one and a half meters. She must weigh barely fifty kilos. You have long
hair, she wears it short. Brunettes, both. Black eyes for you, brown for
her. You both are very cute. You both have very pretty bodies. You have...
Your breasts are very beautiful, I think, we will see that very soon, and the
size of beautiful little melons. Juliette's are very pretty, but very small and
insolent. Your vest still hides your butt from us... You must have a superb
ass, which goes very well with your breasts. Our little Juliette has a little
ass that matches her little tits. Ah... Pubes both shaved. Do you have any
questions, my dear?

During this entire tirade, Laury was massaging the

shoulders of Juliette, paralyzed, and I wondered what this
comparison meant. Juliette ends up answering him.

- No Laury...

- Perfect... To finish with our little Juliette... She is attached to a large
varnished wooden X. Arms raised, spread, and legs apart. Juliette is a real
naughty girl. She lives... Let's say she comes from quite a distance away.
And that she is therefore not Breton. She traveled a long way, only to find
herself tied, naked to a wooden cross and in front of an audience... Don't
you think?

- If Laury...

- Well it's quite simply because our charming guest is a real slut. A
very submissive little whore, who loves being exhibited in public.

Exhibited, humiliated, spanked, whipped... Anyway! Our little bitch likes to be submissive and punished by people like us. I even believe that his next session will pay off. Oh yes... Just to make her feel like a real whore. A little whore, paid, after we used her.

Laury had taken Juliette's hand again, and she allowed herself to be guided without putting up any resistance. His fingers approached me, until they touched me.

- His throat... A red leather dog collar... There, you follow the leash that hangs from his neck... Red leather too...

Juliette's hand roamed my body, and I couldn't help but think of what she was doing with Juliette, in their privacy. To what the three of us had even done, virtually, certain evenings which still haunt my memories. But I don't think Juliette had made the connection yet.

- Nipple clamp on the right breast, Laury told him... Gently pull on it... There you go...

I felt Juliette's breath on my skin. I wanted her. She was stretching my breast, and I started to grimace.

- Nipple clamp, the left... Shoot! Again... Pull gently until this little whore screams...

Juliette hesitated. His fingers brushed my left breast, which instantly swelled. The tip rose, just as Juliette began to pull on the pliers, until I couldn't hold back a cry of pain.

Satisfied, Laury made Juliette bend over, to guide her hand between my thighs.

- A thread... And what is at the end of this thread, my dear?
- I don't know Laury.
- A vibrating egg... It's one of everyone's favorite toys.

our little whore...

While speaking, Laury pulled on Juliette's vest and bared her shoulders. The wool slipped down her arms, revealing her superb chest, and ended up on the floor. Juliette was naked, and despite my fear, the desire for this girl overwhelmed me. Laury took her hand again, leading it to my little ass.

- Do you know where your hand is, my dear?
- Yes I believe Laury...
- Or so ?
- On a buttock...

Laury pulled her hair with such force that the pain made Juliette turn pale.

- You didn't say the magic word...
- Sorry Laury...

- Run your fingers through the crack of this whore's buttocks...
This time, the insult filled me with shame, but Juliette's fingers sliding skillfully and sensually between my two tight globes made me melt. She discovered the Rosebud, which adorned my rosette.

- She wears a Laury plug...
- Well done... Do you like wearing one?
- Yes Laury...

But it was now Juliette's pretty ass that Laury was interested in. His hand caressed her buttocks, and I saw his fingers insinuate themselves between them, and circle around her little dark carnation.

Juliette felt the woman's hand caress her buttock and her fingers insinuate between her firm globes. She blushed with shame when Laury ran her fingers over her anus.

- Can I Juliette, asked Laury?
- Yes Laury... she replied, blushing.
Immediately, our hostess stuck her finger between the

Juliet's kidneys. Slowly, deeply.

I glanced at the giant screen, and saw a mosaic of images. Each had to correspond to the groups which would benefit from the spectacle of our antics this evening. One of them caught my attention: two women... One was, undoubtedly, Yvette. Next to her... a tall blonde... Juliette!

- You have a very welcoming ass, my dear. I won't forget it.

Laury fingered her with the skill no doubt given to her by long experience. I imagined how delicious it was, especially for me who loves anal sex.

- I'm going to give our little whore my finger to suck, announced Laury, removing it from Juliette's pretty ass.

I turned pale. I had always refused Juliette to suck my finger when she demanded that I search my little hole. But there I was stuck. I wasn't going to say the word that would end everything so quickly...

I accepted this new humiliation. I parted my mouth, and his middle finger came to rest on my tongue. Was it the excitement? I barely felt disgust.

- That's because the naughty girl likes it... Suck it well, slut!

Laury took Juliette's hand again, and directed it between my torn thighs. The fingers of the pretty brunette met the string of my vibrating egg.

- You pull gently... I'll start the egg.

Juliette obeyed him, and a slight noise emanated from the egg, which soon returned to my pussy, vibrating. For my greatest pleasure.

- Thank you Juliette. Well... It's time to get down to business. Gentlemen! You can punish our little vicious girl. She must be getting impatient because her pussy is dripping wet.

The three men stood up, and my heart sank at the sight of the light I saw in their eyes. I barely realized what was happening to Juliette.

Laury had grabbed a collar and a leash, similar to mine, and said to my companion in misfortune:

- A pretty dog collar, black and decorated with red stones. And a matching leash. Have you ever been on a leash Juliette?

- No Laury...
- Never ?
- Never Laury...

- Oh it's perfect! It's very exciting ! Said Laury, pinching poor Juliette's hardened nipple, with a sardonic laugh. You are going to be a very beautiful dog Juliette. Come on ! On all fours !

But I didn't have time to see what happened to Juliette. Simon, Vincent and Timothée were now very close to me, and what I had before my eyes terrified me.

Chapter 7

I FOUND MYSELF FACING the three men. The blonde held a whip, with long black leather straps, while the dark-haired man with imposing muscles held a large riding crop, ending in a strand of leather, with which he played while giving me a wicked smile.

Terrified, I saw my black driver approach and untie my ankles. He untied my wrists too, but it was to make me turn around, and present my back and my buttocks. Immediately, I found myself tied up, torn apart.

- You're going to do exactly what I tell you, you little whore, he told me. Any disobedience on your part will see the blows intended for you redouble. Is that understood, Juliette?

  - Yes...
  - Call me Master!

 - Yes... Master, I hastened to add, to avoid his anger.

  - You like being hit, humiliated, don't you?
  - Yes Master.

- So, you will be served. We'll take care of your little titties and your pretty ass first.

The black man accelerated the movements of the egg which was still vibrating in my juicy little apricot. He took between his fingers the tip of my right breast, crushed by the pliers, and began by stretching and twisting it. I bit my lip to keep from screaming, but he insisted until a muffled moan escaped me.

- Go ahead, he ordered the other two.

Immediately, I felt the straps of the flogger and the whip lashing my back and my buttocks. The blows rained down, in series.

- Do you like that, slut, Timothée regularly asked me?

- Yes, Master, I had to answer each time.

And each time, the force of the blows redoubled, the egg vibrated more and more strongly in my cave flooded with wet. The sensations it gave me were exacerbated by the presence of the plug which dilated my little hole. I felt like I was going to cum, but I didn't want to show it. I had not yet completely gotten over my feeling of shame.

And then, I lost my footing, and I gave in to an orgasm of incredible violence. Fortunately, the violence of the whip and whip blows at that moment allowed me to attribute my cries to pain.

My torturers didn't seem to notice that I had cum, too busy whipping me. They decided to make me change position, and I took advantage of this short respite to look at Juliette.

The pretty brunette was kneeling between Laury's thighs who, with her skirt rolled up, held her by the hair, and forced her to search her pussy with her fingers. I almost envied him.

In a few seconds, I was tied back to the cross, facing the three men. Timothée took a nipple clamp again, and pulled it so hard that I thought he was going to tear off my nipple, and I screamed.

- Take care of her pretty little tits, he said to Simon, the blond one, while holding my erect nipple. I felt THE thongs of swift touch there birth of my breasts, go down to caress the underside of the two globes. I was trembling with fear, waiting THE blows Who born would be missed not to arrive. I saw Simon cock his arm, and the leather straps came to bite my chest, very close to the erect nipples, where it is most sensitive. They wrapped around my breasts, and I screamed at every shot.

Timothée, the black guy, passed his fingers between my thighs, and showed them off, glistening with my love juice.

- You did see ? She's wet! She likes it ! Right, Juliet? Are you a real submissive slut?

- Yes, Master, I like That. I am your slut submitted.

- Then you'll love what's next!

I suffered even more from the shame of being humiliated and taking pleasure in it, than from the blows I received. Timothée grabbed my ankles, lifted them off the ground, and removed the vibrating egg from my pussy. I found myself hanging by the wrists from the cross, legs apart, and Vincent approached, while the straps of the swift continued to streak my breasts with red marks.

The wick of the crop traveled for a long time between my thighs, especially on the inside, where the skin is the softest and most sensitive. She sometimes ventured onto my pussy, spreading my lips, to make sure I was wet. I couldn't hide it. At moment Or I me there was waiting THE less, there

The whip came to sting the inside of my thighs. One and the other alternately. Going back to my parted labia majora. My screams rose in pitch, following the progression of the whip. Vincent started by aiming at my lower stomach, just above my little slit. I was writhing in pain, but also in pleasure. And my cries became howls, at the moment when the bit of the riding crop bit my little button.

I thought I was going to get a short break, because the trio moved aside. I was very wrong. Timothy told me that my punishment would only end when I had climaxed.

- Tell me you agree, that you like being punished and that you are going to cum.

- Oh, Master... It hurts too much, I replied, sincerely doubting that I would ever reach orgasm again.

- This is not what I want! You will cum, if you want us to stop!

- Yes Master, I'm going to cum.

- Say it loudly: I want to be punished, until I enjoy admitting it.

- Yes... I want to be punished. I'll tell you that I'm enjoying it.

Maxime approached me with his camera. Looking down, I saw the marks of the flogger and the riding crop on my chest, my stomach, and my thighs.

Timothée and his blond friend grabbed my ankles, and lifted my spread legs square, higher than my face. Maxime filmed me close-up, from every angle. He zoomed in on my face, grimacing with pain and pleasure, my makeup ruined by my tears, my breasts pinched, the marks of the whippings. I was drenched in sweat, and I felt my wetness dripping down my thighs and onto my sore buttocks. I couldn't catch my breath.

Timothée opened my poor little pussy with his fingers, to offer the camera my parted labia, my darting clit, and my slit from which my love juice continued to flow freely.

- Look at the screen bitch, he ordered me!

I turned my head towards the giant screen, and I discovered the spectacle I was offering, in spite of myself. And at the bottom of the screen, the small windows where we could see the reactions of the virtual "guest" couples of this evening. The pride of showing myself off like this helped me bear the shame and humiliation of letting myself be treated like this.

- Aren't you ashamed of getting wet like that in front of everyone?

- If...
- If what !
- I am ashamed !
- Do you like being punished slut?
- Yes I like to be punished...

In this position, I was completely vulnerable. The crop fell on my soaked penis, and I began to scream continuously. I twisted and struggled under the blows, until I no longer felt my wrists attached to the cross.

It was Timothée who was hitting me now, with formidable skill and precision. The long leather strap slammed on my pussy, but also between my spread buttocks, and on my little hole dilated by my anal jewel;

- Cum, little whore, he told me regularly. Cum if you want me to stop.

- I can't... Please, I replied from time to time.

But I knew I was lying, and for my part

great shame, the pleasure was starting to make me lose all restraint. It was no longer just the pain that made me arch and buck.

- It's coming... It's coming... I ended up admitting, sobbing.

- What's coming bitch?

I couldn't answer. I continued to scream, but finally, I spoke the words demanded of me, sealing my defeat.

- I'm going to cum soon!
- Repeat bitch!
- I'm going to cum soon!
- Stronger !

- I'M GONNA CUM!.... I'm enjoying... OOOOOOh! I'M CUMMING!!!

Spasms of crazy, unspeakable pleasure paralyzed me, carried me away, until I almost lost consciousness. Jets of wet spurted from my tortured pussy, while I continued to utter inarticulate cries, interspersed with "Fuck, oh fuck!" It's good ! ". And thinking that seven couples were watching me on their screens made my enjoyment even more complete.

Timothée untied me and put me back on my feet, but I couldn't stand on my still trembling legs. I couldn't catch my breath, and my whole body was shaking.

While the blond freed me from my clamps and my plug, I saw Juliette, licking Laury's pussy, obviously in heaven. But Timothée didn't give me time to enjoy the scene, and seeing that I was recovering a little, he barked:

- You know where the bathroom is!
- Yes...
- Then you come back and sit down.

Chapter 8

I TOOK MY TIME SHOWERING. My body was sore, and the cool water running over my skin soothed the twinges and tingles that reminded me of the treatment I had just undergone.

But my mind was not at rest. How could I have gotten to this point? Exhibited, humiliated, brutalized, but finding perverse pleasure in this situation in which I had put myself. There was indeed this word, which we had agreed with Laury, and which would allow me to stop everything. Only, I wanted to say it less and less. I wanted to push my fantasies and my limits to the limit, to prove myself.... Prove what to me? I didn't even know it!

I decided to return to the large room, knowing that other trials awaited me there. I obeyed Timothée's last order, and I returned to sit, naked, on a sofa, where I found Juliette. Her mask had been taken off, and she could now see me.

She looked at me with a curious eye, without

recognize. It's true that, in the photos of me that she had seen, I had carefully hidden my face, and everything that would have allowed me to be recognized. And she probably didn't expect to find me here, so far from home.

I was drinking water from the neck of a bottle when the blond approached me, holding the collar and leash that Laury had given me when I arrived. He fixed me with a hard look, and I decided to anticipate his order, fearing further punishment.

I knelt down, and he fixed the collar around my neck, before hooking the leash to it. I got on all fours, and followed him when he started to move forward.

Timothée walked towards Juliette, with the same accessories. When he held out the necklace towards her, she barely paused. Like me, she got on all fours, and let herself be tied up like a dog.

The two men led us to Laury, who was staring at the giant screen. My gaze stopped on the images passing through the different windows, and suddenly I saw Yvette and Juliette.

Yvette had put the sound on, muted until now, and on an order from Laury, Maxime intervened so that their video went to full screen.

- Hello, said Yvette to the other couples, some of whom were already naked.

Everyone responded to her, and congratulated her on her initiative. Yvette let out a loud laugh when a man told her that he found the spectacle they offered with Juliette charming. Judging by the expression on the latter's face, she was less enthusiastic...

- Come on, my dear, Yvette told her... I want some pleasure...

- Yvette...

- Get on your knees and lick me!
- You want me to beg you...

Juliette spoke in a voice choked with embarrassment, and her eyes implored her friend, who seemed determined to subject her to the worst outrages.

- You will satisfy my every whim. Starting with this one... I didn't take a shower this morning. I do not really know why. A desire to laze around... If you hadn't called me, I would have been in the shower. But your phone call excited me and gave me this idea. And you know why ? I know you hate not being all clean. But you're going to do it with me. You're going to lick me in the state I'm in. I'm dying for it. And you're going to get wet like the slut you are... Obey now!

Yvette got up and undressed completely, in a few sensual gestures. She remained standing in front of her webcam, and exposed herself for a moment for the other voyeurs, before sitting down on her sofa. She spread her thighs wide, and shamelessly offered view her heavy pear-shaped breasts and the red hair of her pussy.

- Come on, she said to Juliette, while playing with the erect tips of her breasts.

She pressed on Juliette's head, to force her to lick it. She pulled on her blond hair, and the one I had so often called "Mistress" lent herself to all of Yvette's demands. We could guess, from the movements of her head, and from the reactions of the redhead, what she was doing. And so that the voyeurs of this evening have no doubt, she briefly turned Juliette's face towards the webcam, offering us the spectacle of her lips and her chin sticky with thick love juice.

- My friends... Juliette is doing it wonderfully. It won't be long before I cum... Lick me well my darling...

Juliette's head plunged back between her thighs

of Yvette, who raised her legs high. I understood that she was having her carnation licked, and I glanced furtively at Juliette: she was visibly moved to see her wife being treated in this way, even if it was her who had delivered to Laury and his acolytes.

Suddenly, Yvette pulled Juliette's blonde locks, ordering her not to move. She lifted her skirt, exposing her bare buttocks to the webcam, which caused one of the spectators to shout to say that he found the scene arousing.

- I will take off her thong later, Yvette replied. Patience !

Then she started pinching her nipples again, spreading her thighs even wider.

- Lick me quickly slut! Quickly ! I'm going to cum... Juliette followed the movements imposed on her

Yvette. She was licking her slit, and you could hear the wet noises caused by the back and forth movements of her tongue. She had stuck two fingers, coated with love juice, into the redhead's little hole, and was fingering her furiously.

This sight had made me forget my own situation, and I got wet looking at Juliette's pretty ass.

It was then that Yvette uttered a long, hoarse moan.

- I'm coming...I'm cumming!

Yvette squirted, contracting spasmodically under the effects of the orgasm that shook her. Juliette continued to suck her clit, and drink the juice that spilled from the redhead's open cunt.

But I saw Laury turn towards Juliette and me, and I understood that it was our turn to once again offer the spectacle of our submission.

Chapter 9

Chapter 9

L aury addressed the voyeurs, who had to watch us again at home, on their screens.

- Maxime told me that for some of you, this break has been very profitable. I will be sure to watch what happened, don't doubt it...

Then she continued, brushing my hair:

- I promised you a pleasant show... So I will keep my promise!

Laury was now stroking Juliette's hair

- Don't you find our two submissives adorable? And above all terribly exciting? Aren't our two dogs superb?

Juliette and I remained motionless, on all fours, waiting, anxiously, for what would come next.

— For Juliette, who I'm currently caressing... A Great Dane is a natural choice. For our little whore... I hesitated. Small, petite... I thought of a greyhound. A doggy style! Aren't they both beautiful female dogs? A pretty fine and distinguished greyhound. A superb, robust and well-shaped Danish harmonious.

Laury ordered the two men who had us on a leash to come closer to her, and we advanced on all fours, pulled by our collars.

- We will now let our female dogs get to know each other... Gentlemen!

For the first time, our faces were very close to each other. I found Juliette particularly beautiful. Juliette was right when she said that she was hot, and despite the fear that gripped me, I had a crazy desire for her.

- Your tongues, Timothy cried.

This time, the black man's order anticipated my own desire. My lips found those of Juliette, moved and disturbed by the spectacle of his wife, subjected to Yvette's perversity. His mouth opened, to allow passage for my tongue, in search of his, for a fiery kiss. But Juliette didn't completely abandon herself, not as much as I hoped.

- Doggy style! Lick Dane's face, Timothée barked!

I literally rushed towards Juliette. My wet mouth, my tongue ran over the pretty features of her face, like a female dog would have done.

I went beyond orders, and the bite on my buttocks from the flogger, handled by the blond, accompanied by a sharp smack, reminded me that I needed to be gentler. I hastened to obey... But this "sequence" was too short-lived for my liking.

- On your knees Danish! Look good, shouted Timothée, who was holding Juliette's leash.

He pulled the leash upwards, accompanying his order with a violent blow of the crop which slashed her buttocks, and made her cry out.

- Obey! On your knees and hands in the air!

Juliette was now in front of me, kneeling,

arms raised. On an order from the black guy, punctuated by a stroke of the crop on her chest, she spread her muscular thighs. Under the effect of humiliation, her face had turned red, and I could tell from her bright eyes that she was holding back tears.

- Lick her tits, you little whore, my master ordered me.

I admit that I loved receiving this order, and that obeying it excited me terribly.

Also kneeling in front of Juliette, very close to her, I first attacked her right breast. My tongue ran over the round, hard globe, and I saw the tip rise. Juliette, despite her shame, visibly appreciated it! As my tongue began to circle around the taut areola, the blond demanded that I take care of his left breast, and I received a tremendous blow from the flogger on my arched buttocks, to encourage me.

I realized that, in that moment, the pain caused by the biting of the leather straps became pleasure. I admitted it to myself, without feeling the slightest remorse.

I started licking Juliette's chest again, with increased enthusiasm. My saliva shone on her dark skin, and the sighs of the pretty brunette testified to her pleasure and her abandonment.

I had attacked the erect nipples, sucking them, sucking them, covering them with the caresses of my tongue, when a volley of strokes fell on my little ass.

- Doggy style! Teeth now, cried Timothy.

I gently bit the swollen buds, as if ready to burst. One after the other. Stretching them gently, until Juliette groaned in pain, to immediately release them, and take them again, to bite them and torment them even more.

I was wet like a real slut. I was not

arrived to wait and desire the blows of the swift, which did not take long to fall. I was impatient to discover the rest, certain that it would lead me to exhibit myself with Juliette, whose moans spoke of the pleasure.

- You all know what two beautiful female dogs do when they want to get to know each other better, Laury commented?

- Danish! Turn around, Timothy shouted.

Juliette blushed again, turned around, and got down on all fours, offering me the magnificent spectacle of her frightening lower back.

- Doggy style! Lick Dane's ass, called out my master.

I stuck my face between the two buttocks, firm and muscular. I was thrilled. The idea of my humiliation no longer even occurred to me. I placed a few light kisses at the birth of the furrow separating these two hemispheres, before my tongue began its exploration. I had wanted this ass so much, in my hot chats with Juliette!

- That's good, Greyhound, my master complimented me.

You are a good female dog.

- Arch your back more, Dane, said Timothée.

Juliette obeyed, with an eagerness which led me to believe that she was taking pleasure in this situation, and in my caresses. To be sure, my tongue went down to her swollen apricot, which I found flooded with love juice. Juliette started to moan, and I started to lick her little hole, faster and faster, harder and harder. I guessed that she was about to cum, and I twisted her puckered eyelet with the tip of my tongue. But I didn't have time to bring her to orgasm.

- Turn around, Greyhound, Simon, the blond one, ordered me. I stood up, and I saw the black guy pull on the leash of Juliette, who allowed herself to be directed.

- Your turn Danish... Eat the little female dog's ass!

My master spread my buttocks with all the force of his powerful hands, and I arched my back, offering my ass to Juliette. I immediately felt his mouth, his tongue, licking my buttocks, even sinking his teeth into it. I couldn't hold back a moan of happiness, Juliette's caresses were so slow and gentle. I began to moan when the tip of his tongue lingered on my rosette, as I had done myself.

- Faster ! Better than that, shouted Timothée, who punctuated each sentence with a tap of his flogger, the sound of which made me jump.

Juliette cried out in pain, but followed her master's order. She began to lick me with uncontrolled ardor. I flowed like a fountain, and the mouth of the pretty brunette wandered over my slit, drinking the thick sticky love juice that hung in trickles from my little lips.

A new stroke of the swift streaked Juliette's back, and she returned to my little hole. His mouth was glued to my puck, which his tongue was exploring.

For a moment, I thought of the voyeurs spying on us on their screens. Especially Juliette. What did she feel, looking at the two of us? "Her" Juliette, on all fours, her pussy exposed, devouring the ass of her submissive little whore?...

- Doggy style, lie on your back, Laury asked me, visibly excited.

I obey, offering my naked body dripping with sweat, my little tits as hard as stone, my thighs spread over my open cunt. Juliette came on top of me, in 69. She began to suck my clit, sucking it greedily.

The pretty brunette's sweating and wetness

were also dripping on me, and my mouth attacked her pussy and her little hole. I writhed under this magnificent body,

We both moaned, on the verge of pleasure. We both tried to delay our orgasm, but suddenly Juliette pushed her tongue so deep into my slit that I could no longer control myself.

I enjoy, writhing with pleasure, in a long cry muffled by Juliette's sex, crushed on my mouth. I wanted her to come too, and I gently bit her little lips. A hoarse moan told me that I had achieved my goals, and a flow of sweet, warm wet flooded my face.

- Again ! Keep going, bitches, Laury shouted to us. I had not abandoned Juliette's beautiful juicy apricot, and I redoubled my ardor to lick and suck it. But the pretty brunette, overcome by pleasure, remained motionless, her plays posed on My belly thrilling.

- Eat it, Dane, the black man ordered her. Obey, female dog!

I heard the hiss of the leather straps, and their snap as they bit Juliette's buttocks. Immediately, Juliette's mouth and tongue invested my gaping slit.

- Keep going, Dane!

The tip of Juliette's tongue gave me indescribable pleasure, twirling around my hard and erect bud. But the blows continued to rain down, on her back and on her pretty ass. I wanted to offer myself more and more to Juliette, and I raised my legs as far apart as possible, revealing my buttocks and my little hole. Juliette's moans rose in pitch, without me knowing if her excitement came from me, or from the thrusts of swift.

Except that now it was obviously going to be my turn to suffer...

Simon let go of my leash and came to kneel between my legs. He kept them apart, and he pushed Juliette's face away. Out of the corner of my eye, I saw a dildo in his hand. Black. Huge ! I should have been afraid, but the course of that evening had made me another woman, drunk with pleasure, ready to accept everything.

I felt the monstrous silicone glans pressing against my little dark eyelet. I held my breath, trying to relax. With little flicks of his wrists, the blond pressed the olisbos against my rosette, which opened slowly. I bit my lips. This thing was too big for my little ass. A twinge of pain surprised me, but I didn't cry out.

And then, almost miraculously, the pain subsided, replaced by the weird sensation I already knew, when my anus is distended, mixing pleasure with the fear of being torn. It was as if my ass had swallowed this glans, and the long black rod began to sink in slowly, while waves of pleasure radiated from the hollow of my buttocks.

- She likes that, our little dog, Simon commented.

Finishing his sentence, he pushed the dildo completely into my little eyelet in one go. My whole body shook with spasms, and I let out a long cry that echoed throughout the room. I realized, when I opened my eyes, that Maxime was circling around us, filming us. Our voyeurs had to have a close-up view of my sodomized ass, and the thought turned me on a little more.

I resumed my cunnilingus, on Juliette's pussy, from where

A clear juice was flowing, and I saw Timothée grab another dildo, undoubtedly similar to the one which was now sodomizing me at a regular rhythm. Juliette didn't suspect anything.

- Arch your back, Dane, he ordered in his bass voice, placing a hand on his buttocks, streaked with dark red marks.

Juliette obeyed, certainly fearing that she would be whipped again. And the black guy began to penetrate her tight little hole, slowly, but without giving her any respite. I saw the resin glans force the narrow sphincter, in small circular movements, until it gave way. Juliette's moans made me flow even more, and did not stop.

- Eat yourselves, female dogs, called Simon, when the whole rod of resin had found its place in Juliette's pretty ass.

I felt the pretty brunette's mouth crash onto my burning vulva, and I began to devour her little darting button again. From that moment on, we both went wild.

My whole body seemed to be concentrated in my little apricot, which Juliette was literally eating. His lips kissed, sucked, sucked my clit with increased sensitivity. His tongue licked my slit, twisting it to penetrate it as deeply as it could. She was drooling, and her saliva flooded my pussy and my thighs, mixing with my wetness.

I responded to each of his attacks. Timothée had left the dildo planted in his female dog's ass, who was contracting while undulating her hips. Like me, she had forgotten all modesty, she had renounced all dignity. We knew that our humiliation and our perversion were being offered as food to a gang of voyeurs, but we no longer felt any shame at being treated like this. On the contrary.

I felt Juliette's hard, erect nipples rubbing against my stomach. Our moans, our inarticulate cries filled the room, and undoubtedly those in which the voyeurs were watching us.

Suddenly, Juliette's teeth planted themselves gently in my apricot. I screamed. She then came, and streams of her juice gushed from her slit, flooding my face. But she did not calm down, squirming harder to experience the hardness of the enormous dildo stuck in her anus.

I delayed my orgasm as much as I could, despite the back and forth of the sex toy filling my little dark eyelet, according to Simon's desires. I continued to devour this pretty cunt, as I had dreamed of for months.

And then, my pleasure came like a tidal wave. I felt carried away, I tensed like a bow, I arched my paralyzed body... I came, with incredible violence, I felt that I was squirting, interminably, shaken by convulsions similar to those of an epileptic.

I barely realized that Juliette was also enjoying, a second time, moaning as if she were dying. Then she fell on top of me, our bodies dripping with sweat rubbing gently against each other, full of tenderness, and her mouth traveled slowly down my stomach, and my still throbbing mound.

I saw Timothée remove the dildo stuck between Juliette's buttocks, and Simon imitated him. It was an empty feeling, almost frustrating, when my little ass was freed from the resin member that had given it so much pleasure.

- Get up, Dane, Timothée ordered the pretty brunette, pulling on her leash.

Chapter 10

Chapter 10

Simon and Timothée took us into a bathroom, looking a bit like the showers in a sports hall. The water gushing from the shower heads flowed onto the tiled floor, before disappearing into a siphon. Maxime, always armed with his camera, followed us and filmed our every move, like a television reporter. But he stopped at the entrance to the bathroom, giving me hope for a moment of (relative) privacy. As to has our two "masters", they se

S tripped down to their black boxers.

I felt a pressing urge to urinate but, although asking the black guy in the most servile tone, this request was rejected.

Our leashes and collars were removed, and we found ourselves side by side, Juliette and I, under the very hot water of the shower. I took the opportunity to say to him, in a low voice:

- You know me, but you didn't recognize me. I'm Juliette23, Juliette's submissive little whore.

- You?... she replied. Your face was masked

in your photos, but yes, this body...

She had no time to continue. Timothée and Simon had joined us, and began to wash us, to the great shame of Juliette, who could barely contain herself.

They began by soaping us abundantly, covering us with a soft and creamy foam. They groped us, as if we were objects or slaves. It was first our faces, stained with the remains of our makeup, our necks, our shoulders, our armpits that sweat made sticky, which were allowed to be methodically washed.

Juliette's long brown hair covered her eyes, and she remained inert, while Timothée kneaded her chest, but the erection of her nipples betrayed her. For my part, I appreciated being treated like this. I had resigned myself to being a slut subject to the whims of Simon – of Laury too, of all the others – and I took a perverse pleasure in it, much more than I would have ever imagined.

Simon's hand moved down to my stomach, and I couldn't hold back a sigh of contentment. But Juliette had a start at the contact of Timothée's fingers on her mound of Venus.

- No, she exclaimed, stiffening, and stepping back.

- Hygiene is essential, Timothée replied, without violence.

- I'll do it myself, said Juliette, who regained her pride for a moment.

The black man smiled, and remained silent for a moment. Then his features regained their usual hardness.

- So I think the evening will end for you! You shouldn't even talk to me. You are there for the pleasure of the guests... So?

But Juliette did not calm down, and she took another step back.

- And what are you? A stooge or a guest, she called out to Timothée.

I admired his courage and his character. There was a slight hesitation on the part of both men, and Simon left me to join his sidekick. It was he who spoke.

- Actors in a show. We all have a role to play. Yours is to accept everything.

- We're no longer in the show, Juliette protested more violently.

- You are wrong... I understand your reaction but I assure you that we are making an exception for you. Because it's your first time. We will tell Laury about this moment in detail. And she will repeat it to excite her friends. It is precisely because no one is looking at you at the moment that the story will be very exciting. Submissive to the end. You understand ?

Juliette looked down at Timothée's black boxers, and a faint glint of envy in her eyes did not escape the black man.

- Disappointed? For us too this moment is quite delicate. Although with Juliette...

He pointed at me, like a filly at a cattle fair.

- ... She likes it. It would be much more pleasant for me. You don't like it... If you decide, you'll see something else. And since up until now you have accepted everything...

Juliette fell silent, defeated. Timothée shoved his dark fingers into her pussy to wash her, extracting from her a moan like a wounded animal, and I was entitled to the same treatment. But I loved it, and I no longer even tried to defend myself from it. So I savored this degrading caress, and soon, it was my little hole who suffers the same fate.

When the scalding water ran over our two bodies, to rinse them, I glanced at Juliette secretly. Her hard, swollen breasts and the light that shone in her eyes made me think that she, too, was beginning to experience a pleasure similar to mine.

Simon and Timothée reattached the collars around our necks, and brought us back to the large room, on all fours, pulled by our leashes, leaving behind us the wet traces of our bodies on which the drops of water sparkled.

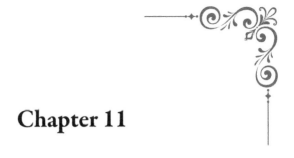

Chapter 11

Chapter 11

Laury looked at us, looking satisfied, and Timothée told her the story of our "toilet", omitting no detail, in particular Juliette's desire to revolt. Timothée repeated and commented on his story, for the benefit of the voyeurs whose images I saw on the giant screen.

Juliette had turned scarlet, and I could guess how embarrassed she was that Juliette learned of her humiliation, even if the jealousy of "his wife" had already been put to the test this evening. Because I had felt, through my exchanges with Juliette, the depth of the loving feeling she felt for Juliette, despite – or because of – their very particular sex life.

As far as I was concerned, I was certain that Juliette was delighted to see me treated like a sex slave, and I suspected her of being at the origin of my presence at this evening.

Laury was standing between Timothée and Simon, and we were both kneeling at her feet, like two obedient female dogs. Our eyes turned to Vincent, the bodybuilder with long black hair, who had remained inactive until then.

He was sitting on a sofa, naked, allowing his imposing muscles to be admired, but it was the sight of Maxime that surprised me. The latter was on his knees between his thighs, and he was sucking Vincent's erect cock.

Laury contemplated the scene with an amused expression, before saying to Timothée and Simon:

- Undress me !

They hastened to obey the mistress of the evening. The two men took off his suit. Underneath, she only wore the bra, which I had glimpsed, a lace thong, and a garter belt which held up her black stockings. She was round, but unabashedly wore these shapes that suited her perfectly, and I found her beautiful.

- Look at me, she ordered Juliette and me.

Simon popped the clasp on her bra, and her heavy breasts sank a little, even though they were hard with arousal.

- Help me take off my thong, you little whore, she said.

In fact, it was me who slid the elastic over her hips and down her thick thighs, and Juliette had to pick up the little triangle of lace that had fallen to the floor.

Laury was only wearing her garter belt, stockings and pumps. She then walked towards a sofa, opposite the one where Vincent was seated, and called us in a soft voice. We joined her, on all fours, before kneeling at her feet, while Simon and Timothy, dressed, placed themselves on each side of the seat, as sentries would have done.

- Vincent..., called Laury.

The dark-haired bodybuilder looked up at her, and Maxime interrupted his fellatio.

- Sodomize him, she added, pointing to Maxime with a contemptuous movement of her chin.

Maxime seemed ashamed to submit, too, before our eyes, but this prospect did not seem to frighten him. He took off his jacket, just before Vincent grabbed him, and forced him to bend over, his arms and face on the sofa cushions. Suddenly, Vincent lowered his pants, which fell to his ankles.

I was mesmerized by this scene. Vincent jerked off, to bring his penis to a full erection. He spread Maxime's buttocks, and without further preparation, he fucked him, extracting a cry of pain from him.

Huddled against me, Juliette was stunned. Vincent's muscular buttocks came and went, to the rhythm of his cock strokes in Maxime's forced anus, who was uttering plaintive moans. Laury seemed to delight in this spectacle, but she turned towards us.

- Come closer, my darlings.

She was seated, half lying down, her neck resting against the backrest, her buttocks on the edge of the sofa, her feet placed on the cushions. Her fleshy thighs were spread wide, over her already wet pussy.

- Do me good, my darlings.

Juliette and I plunged our heads into the crook of Laury's legs. We shared her swollen, juicy apricot, taking turns kissing and licking it. We devoured her little button out of her hood, our tongues insinuated into her open cave.

I took advantage of this proximity to try to kiss Juliette. She pressed her lips against mine, while I caressed Laury so that she don't notice it.

- You excite me, I said in a low voice to the pretty brunette.

But I had to start attacking Laury's cunt again, nibbling her turgid bud. Long growls reflected his excitement, and waves of wet stained my face, and that of Juliette.

She, sweating, stood up to pull back her wet hair which was bothering her, and she remained on her knees, forgetting to satisfy her mistress.

Laury had opened the flies of Simon and Timothée, freeing their sexes, which she was slowly wanking. Juliette couldn't take her eyes off the two erected stakes. Especially Timothée's, dark, shiny, thick... a real ebony club.

He caught her gaze, and Juliette closed her eyes when she saw his gesture. The crop fell on his buttocks with a sharp crack.

- Danish! He scolded her in his bass voice.

Laury took me by the hair, to push my mouth between her buttocks, and Juliette's tongue sank into her open and juicy fruit.

Vincent's voice pulled Laury from seeking her pleasure.

- He has his account, he says, speaking of Maxime.
- Did he cum, Laury asked him in a broken voice?
- Look. His cum spurted all over the floor.
- Oh ! The pig !

The ejaculation of her sodomized companion, far from disturbing Laury, excited her even more. She grabbed our hair, placing our mouths on her pussy and her dark rosette, and began to undulate her hips again. Until she came, interminably, moaning, and squirting all over our faces.

Then she gently pushed us away, and remained still, long enough to regain her senses. She still held Simon and Timothée's cocks in her hands, and she gently scratched their pouches. They were hard like bulls in heat. Juliette and I couldn't take our eyes off these two male sexes, and our eyes went from one to the other, and Laury noticed it.

- Little curious people! Gentlemen! I think your female dogs want your cocks... Get sucked a little!

The two men pulled on our leashes to bring us towards them, still on our knees. I didn't have to be asked to take Simon's cock in my mouth, regretting a little not to be in Juliette's place, to taste Timothée's, more impressive.

Given what I knew about Juliette, her lack of attraction to men, I wondered how she would react. But one glance in his direction me allowed of see it, wanking there long dark shaft, eyes glistening with excitement, before taking the enormous pink glans between her lips. We were sucking our two masters, with relish, when Laury stopped us.

- Oh... I have an idea to punish these vicious little female dogs... Stop it, my darlings!

She looked at us, caressing herself, and stretching a large, darting nipple between her fingers. Juliette blushed.

- The first to please her master will be rewarded. A large bowl of fresh water and some biscuits. The loser will be punished!

I literally threw myself on Simon's penis, while Juliette seemed destabilized, panicked. The fear of losing, no doubt, mixed with the fear of not being up to the task, faced with a lover too experienced, she who had little practice with men..

But she pulled herself together, and took Timothée's hand to guide it to her slit, without saying anything. He started fingering her, and she started sucking the black guy, staring into his eyes. A wet noise rose from Juliette's pussy. She was getting wet. His master took his head in his hands, to guide his movements, and the improbable happened.

- My female dog won, announced Timothée, while he emptied himself in long jets into Juliette's mouth.

She nevertheless continued to pump her master's penis, which she squeezed convulsively between her fingers, to swallow all of his semen. Then she pulled away from him, a long stream of cum running down the corner of her lips.

I looked at Juliette, incredulous, but happy for her.

But an unexpected event disrupted the course of the evening...

Chapter 12

Chapter 12

While I was still playing with Simon's erection, the chime of the front door echoed in the large living room.

- What could possibly come to disturb us at this hour, before the end of this evening, Laury stormed. Maxime, go open!

Maxime had gotten dressed again, and he headed towards the entrance. We heard the sound of voices, and he reappeared very quickly, sheepish, accompanied by a tall, very beautiful blonde woman, whom Juliette looked at with an incredulous expression.

- Laury, excuse me for bothering you during your evening, said the intruder, in a firm voice. I am Juliette. I'm coming to pick up Juliette.

- But... we're not done with her, objected Laury, who seemed not to be bothered in the least by receiving her almost naked.

- That's why I'm here. I made a huge mistake entrusting her to you to punish her, and...

Laury didn't let her finish, and took her aside,

so that we don't hear their conversation. Juliette had barely looked at me, and I regretted it. I would have loved for her to see me naked, "for real". And I was frustrated when I read the love she had for him in Juliette's eyes.

- Juliette, you can go take a shower and get dressed, Laury announced as she came back towards us.

The hostess of this evening had difficulty hiding her annoyance, and while the pretty brunette headed towards the bathroom, she returned to exchange a few remarks – apparently unfriendly – with Juliette.

When Juliette came out of the bathroom, her hair wet, she had put on the large woolen cardigan she wore when she arrived, under which she was still naked, and her boots. Juliette took her by the shoulder, in a protective gesture, and the couple left, without a goodbye.

Laury watched them leave, then turned to me.

- This incident doesn't change anything for you, Greyhound. Except you find yourself alone. You're going to get your punishment, and we're going to treat you like a little whore. I know you like it. Gentlemen, take care of her!

I cast a panicked look in the direction of Timothée, Vincent, and Simon, who were observing me like prey.

I was alone, facing them...

Chapter 13

Chapter 13

SIMON TOOK MY LEASH again and led me to the middle of the room, facing the giant screen. Laury settled comfortably on a sofa, opening her raised thighs to be able to caress herself easily, and Maxime took back the camera, with which he was going to film the entire scene, like those which had preceded it.

On the screen, I saw, in the different windows, the voyeurs who were still going to delight in my torture. Among them was Yvette, now alone. I no longer knew whether I should hate or thank this woman for what I was suffering through her fault.

Everyone had their eyes glued to their screen, and the idea of showing myself off in front of them made me wet, despite my fear.

And my punishment began...

- You're going to suck us, Simon said in a harsh voice. All three. And you're going to try to do it better than you did with me just now.

He punctuated his sentence with a resounding slap, and I felt a burn on my cheek, while Vincent took the tips of my breasts between his fingers, and twisted them. I couldn't hold back a cry of surprise and pain, which made Laury laugh, immediately stifled by Timothée's cock, which he had planted in my mouth, pulling my hair.

I started to suck him, like a real slut, accepting to receive his enormous penis all the way to the back of my throat. His stake came and went between my lips, he fucked my mouth, as if it had been my pussy.

- But she's doing it well, this female dog, he said. You should have unloaded in her mouth, Simon, she must like cum.

I left Timothy's rod for a moment to catch my breath, but Simon slapped me again and grabbed my hair so that I could suck him too. And just as I took the blond's glans between my lips to nibble it, I felt the leather of a riding crop bite the skin of my poor little sore ass. It was Vincent, encouraged by Laury.

- Go ahead, Vincent. Take good care of her, she will be even hotter when you fuck her.

The worst part is that she wasn't wrong. I was in a daze. The torture inflicted on my buttocks and my breasts, the humiliations I suffered, instead of revolting, excited me beyond anything I could have imagined. I flowed like a fountain. My nipples were tighter than ever.

I sucked Vincent with redoubled energy, searching in my imagination for all the possible variations of fellatio.

Then each of the three men demanded "his due", taking turns in my mouth, pulling my hair, slapping me, while Maxime circled around me, filming me from all angles. Those I wasn't sucking were attacking my breasts, pulling them spikes, twisting them, or whipping me with whips. I moaned when they hurt me too much, but not for a moment did it occur to me to ask them to stop.

I was drunk with desire. I wanted these three guys to fuck me, to take me wildly. If I hadn't been gagged by these imposing cocks, I would have begged them, like a female dog in heat. That's what I was, at that moment.

Then I was allowed a very short respite. He allowed me to see Laury fingering herself, her hands between her thighs, forcefully opening her gaping penis. On the screen, I also saw Yvette, in approximately the same position. As for the couples of voyeurs, their eyes were fixed on me. Including a couple, the man sodomizing his partner, doggy style.

But this pause didn't even last a minute.

Timothée lay down on one of the sofas, his stake raised like the mast of a sailboat. This enormous dark machine fascinated me, as if I were the prey of a reptile. The dark-haired bodybuilder grabbed me, and carried me to him, without me touching the ground. They placed me on top of him, while Vincent slowly jerked off while looking at me with a lustful expression.

Timothée spread my buttocks, and guided his glans engorged with blood towards my little puckered eye, while Vincent let me go down, so that I could impale myself. I screamed when the huge cock forced my tight rosette, but my tormentors didn't care.

Vincent came on top of me, and penetrated me with a single thrust. At the same time, I felt the black man's powerful hands grab my hips, to make me move on the dick that pierced my little ass, and I started to scream. It was painful. But it was so good.

To shut me up, Vincent planted his cock in my

mouth. I was taken in every hole, filmed, to excite a gang of voyeurs. Without admitting it to myself, I had always dreamed of finding myself in this situation, and of taking pleasure in being humiliated. An orgasm paralyzed me, and I began to howl like a wild animal.

My partners were incredibly resilient. When fatigue made me weaken, Vincent would pull my hair, slap me, pinch my breasts which the excitement made horribly sensitive.

Then they exchanged places. Vincent fucked my ass, Simon fucked my pussy, and Timothée my mouth. Sweat was streaming down my face and on my bruised body, lacerated with whip blows, and the wet welled up from my slit with a humid noise, to drip down between my buttocks and down my thighs.

I heard a hoarse moan, and I saw Laury, her head turned towards me, her eyes rolled back, enjoying herself. A trickle of saliva ran down the corner of her lips, and the sofa was soaked between her thighs.

Then the three men exchanged places again. Everyone thus tasted the pleasure of exploring each of my orifices. I was nothing more than an object, a sex toy that they used as they pleased.

They felt that I was also going to cum again, and they went even more wild. My slit and my little hole were painful, and despite that, I came inexorably. This last orgasm left me exhausted, on the verge of passing out, and my moans turned into a weak, uninterrupted moan.

Timothée withdrew from my pussy, and he lifted me, so that I could free myself from Simon's member, still stuck in the hollow of my back. When he let go of me, I didn't have the strength to get back on my feet.

legs, and I collapsed on the ground. But Laury didn't consider me punished enough yet.

- Cover her with cum, this little whore, she shouted to the three men.

Vincent gave me a few blows with the whip until I squatted down, and they again presented me with their three hard members, glistening with my juice. Overcoming my weakness, I began to suck them again, but I didn't have long to wait...

Simon ejaculated first, with a long, hoarse groan. He had delayed this moment so long that the stream of thick, hot cum that gushed from his cock seemed like it would never run dry. I couldn't get everything into my mouth, and I found my face and breasts smeared with a whitish cream.

Vincent followed him, and I almost choked when the jet of cum flooded my throat. He finished on my cheeks, and long tears of his juice continued to flow down my neck, when Timothée relieved himself in turn. He disdained my mouth, and stained my breasts, reddened by the blows, and my stomach.

I thought I was even, but Laury gave him a little sign, which the other two men also understood.

They grabbed me firmly by the shoulders, forcing me to stay crouched; then Timothée took a whip, and while Maxime was filming me in close-up, he ordered me:

- Piss, Doggystyle. Piss on the ground in front of us, and in front of everyone who looks at you.

My bladder felt like it was about to burst, but I couldn't accept this latest humiliation. I was dead of shame. I almost shouted the word that would end everything, but I couldn't remember it because I was so exhausted and mortified.

- No, I only shouted. Noooo! I can't !

- You will obey, Timothée roared, giving me a volley of lashes.

Tears were streaming down my cheeks, carrying some of the cum which was beginning to dry. Vincent had spread my thighs, so that Maxime didn't miss anything of the scene.

- No ! Pity ! I beg you !

- You agreed to be submissive. Until the end. Piss little slut, the black guy yelled, whipping me harder.
- No, no, I still murmured weakly, but everything changed suddenly, in my head, with the last bites of the leather straps.

I was going to give in. But the worst thing was that I felt the pleasure building, despite my shame. Or because of her. I held back for a few more seconds, and I completely surrendered
- I obey, I said to stop my torment. I'm going to pee ! Stop, I'm going to pee.

When the first stream of urine gushed between my thighs, an improbable orgasm took me by surprise. I was breaking all the limits I had ever set for myself.

- I'm cumming I'm cumming oooooh I'm cumming, I sobbed.

I was peeing, unable to stop. My golden liquor splashed my thighs, and mixed with my love juice, flooded the ground, soaking my knees.

Laury, who was tormenting her clit and searching her little hole with four of her fingers, exploded almost at the same time as me, mixing her cries with my moans.

The three men let go of me, and I remained there, on my knees, panting, barely aware of my posture and the state of my body. My tears continued to flow, and after a few minutes, it was Laury who made me stand up again, and who led me into the bathroom, supporting myself.

She had taken off her garter belt, her stockings, her pumps. She was completely naked, and I felt the hard tips of her heavy breasts, crushed against my back.

She turned on the tap, and the very hot water flowed over my skin, streaked by the straps of the whip and the riding crop. My breasts still hurt. My slit and my little hole were burning, but they had been used so much that I barely felt them.

Laury soaped me, washed me with very gentle gestures, before rubbing me with a lotion and a cream, which made my pain disappear, as if by magic. She was now speaking in my ear, and the softness of her voice was surprising, compared to the confident and authoritative tone she had adopted throughout this evening.

- You were wonderful tonight, Juliette. We had rarely had such an exciting guest, from her first time with us. I hope you enjoyed it too...

It wasn't really a question, but the silence she left begged for a response from me.

What to tell him? I didn't know myself.

I felt like I had crossed a border and found myself in unknown territory. The Juliette who was going to leave this house was not the same as when she arrived. Submissive. The word seemed too weak to me. I had accepted everything, tolerated it, endured it all. And I had to admit to myself that, deep in my being, I had loved this role, that it had excited me, and that I had just experienced an enjoyment surpassing anything that my experiences, however numerous and varied, allowed me to achieve.

- I don't know what to answer you, I ended up saying.

I need to recover, to think.

- Take your time. Call me back if you want, whenever you want. You will always be welcomed.

I got dressed again, in silence. My little linen dress, although sexy, seemed useless to me, and I think I would have returned to my apartment naked if Laury had asked me to.

Timothée took me home. We didn't exchange a word during the ride, but there was no trace of resentment in our silence. The intensity of the moments we had just spent made any comment seem ridiculous.

- Goodbye, Juliette, the black man said simply to me, opening my door, when we arrived. Thank you for the pleasure you gave me. Hope we see you again soon.

- I don't know... Goodbye, Timothée, and thank you too.

To be continued....

END

Also by GEMMA ZAMORA

Juliet's punishment

Milton Keynes UK
Ingram Content Group UK Ltd.
UKHW040833120224
437701UK00001B/100